A Cup of Tea in Pamplona

THE BASQUE SERIES

BOOKS BY ROBERT LAXALT

Sweet Promised Land

A Man in the Wheatfield

Nevada

In A Hundred Graves: A Basque Portrait

Nevada: A History

A Cup of Tea in Pamplona

A CUP OF TEA
IN PAMPLONA

ROBERT LAXALT

Illustrations by George Carlson

RENO: UNIVERSITY OF NEVADA PRESS

Basque Series Editor: William A. Douglass

University of Nevada Press, Reno, Nevada 89557 USA
Copyright © Robert Laxalt 1985. All rights reserved.
Printed in the United States of America

Library of Congress Cataloging-in-Publication Data
Laxalt, Robert, 1921–
    A cup of tea in Pamplona.

    1. Basques—Fiction.   I. Title.
PS3562 . A9525C8   1985   813' . 54   85–16371
ISBN 0-87417-095-8 (alk. paper)
ISBN 0-87417-101-6 (lim. ed. : alk. paper)

For my sister, Marie

I

"*Pasaporte?*"

"Here," said Gregorio.

"Thank you," said the Spanish frontier guard. "What is your destination in Spain?"

"Pamplona," said Gregorio.

"And the reason for your visit?" asked the guard.

"A cup of tea in Pamplona," said Gregorio.

"Ah, yes," said the guard. "Well, it's a fine day for a trip. The weather is very nice now."

"It may change," said Gregorio.

"Do you think so?"

"Who can tell?" shrugged Gregorio.

"I expect you are right," said the guard. "Your passport is quite in order. Oh yes, one thing more."

"Yes?"

"As long as you are going all the way to Pamplona for a cup of tea, you might as well have a cookie, too."

"Thank you," said Gregorio. "I'll consider it."

The Spanish frontier guard in the olive green uniform waited until the long Citroen had disappeared around a bend in the winding road that led into Spain, and then he went inside the customs station. The needle of the barometer on the wall of the little room pointed to good weather. He tapped the glass face with his finger. When the needle stopped quivering, it was lower than it had been before. The Spanish guard allowed himself a wry grin and picked up the telephone to call the French customs station a few miles back up the road.

"*Allo?*"

"Montoya here," said the Spanish frontier guard.

"I thought you might call, *capitán*," said the French frontier guard.

"Then you did recognize him when he went through," said the Spanish guard.

"We nearly missed seeing him," said the French guard. "One of the new men was on duty. But I happened to come out when Gregorio was driving away."

"He said his destination was Pamplona," said the Spanish guard.

"Perhaps yes, perhaps no," said the French guard. "It makes little difference where he goes in Spain. Where and when he chooses to have his men come back into France with contraband is what makes the work for us."

"I understand," said the Spanish guard. "Ours is not an easy career."

"Well, thank you for your cooperation, *capitán*," said the French guard. "I am in your debt."

"One thing more," said the Spanish guard. "The barometer is falling."

There was a sigh on the other end of the line. "I should have expected it," said the French guard. "One thing on top of another. As you say, ours is not an easy career."

Around the bend of the mountain, the long Citroen was parked unobtrusively off the road. On the rim of the mountain above, Gregorio the Basque smuggler lay concealed in a growth of rusted bracken. He was propped on his elbows, his beret pushed back on his head. When the Spanish frontier guard framed in the window of the customs station set down his telephone, Gregorio lowered his binoculars. In unhurried succession, he cursed the Spanish frontier guard in Spanish and the French frontier guard further up the mountain in French. Then, for his own satisfaction he cursed in Basque all the telephones in the world. He would have gone on to include the memory of the man who had invented the telephone, except that he did not know his name.

Gregorio the Basque smuggler did not go on to Pamplona. Once he had passed below the timberline of the Pyrenees mountains, he turned off the main highway. The Citroen nosed its way through a leafless Spanish forest and came into a village with a single street. The street divided two rows of stone houses with dingy fronts.

The proprietor of an unmarked restaurant was waiting in the doorway. He was wearing a black beret and a long white apron. "Adio, Gregorio," he said, extending his wrist because his hands were wet.

Gregorio shook him by the wrist. "When are you going to put up a sign? Don't you want to be modern like everybody else?"

The proprietor shrugged amiably. "Why should I put up a sign? Everybody here knows it's a restaurant."

"You're behind the times."

The room inside the doorway was heavy with smoke and gloom. The only light came from a thin slit of window and the low-burning fire. The fireplace was open on all sides, and the hearth extended to the middle of the room.

Gregorio took a seat on one of the narrow benches that surrounded the fire. He was a big man who had been powerful in his youth, and his strength still showed in the sweep of chest beneath his thick tweed coat. Everything about him was gray, from inscrutable gray eyes in a gray face to hair that was more gray than black.

"I could bring you an *aperitivo*," said the proprietor.

"What do you have of interest?" asked Gregorio.

"Wine."

"What do you have for lunch?" asked Gregorio.

"What else? Soup and mutton and salad."

"And wine?"

"Of course, wine."

"I'll wait for Fermin," said Gregorio.

"He will be along," said the proprietor. "He's always late. You know him."

It was a statement of fact that did not deserve an answer, so the smuggler said nothing.

When Fermin came in, Gregorio was contemplating the black maw of a chimney over the fireplace. Fermin had a ruddy face and a moustache with ends that flared out stiffly. He was immensely square and his manner was one of immense dependability. He wore the moustache, which was an oddity in the village, like a dissenting flag of his smuggling profession.

Fermin offered no greeting, but sat down on the bench that slanted off at a right angle from the one on which Gregorio was sitting. After a few minutes, Fermin asked, "Is something bothering you?"

"Yes," said Gregorio. "The United States of Europe."

Fermin regarded him thoughtfully.

"It's coming to that, you know," said Gregorio. "We are getting closer to it every day. Do you know why?"

"No."

"The telephone, that's why."

Fermin began to comprehend. "So they're up to that."

"It's the thing to do," said Gregorio. "Five years ago, I could have rested content knowing that lazy Spaniard would rather fly to the moon than walk five kilometers to the French station to tell them I had passed through. Now all he has to do is pick up the telephone."

"Well, everything changes but the menu," said Fermin.

They went into a dining room that was bare except for a few tables covered with old oilcloth. At one table, four young Basques were talking in low, fierce tones and eating their soup noisily. An old Basque peasant and his wife were eating at another table. They had brought their own lunch but had ordered a bottle of cheap restaurant wine. An entire chicken lay between them on a cloth sack and they were picking at it with their fingers. In the corner of the room, two policemen with sallow Spanish faces were regarding their mutton bleakly. The light from the window glittered off the patent leather straps that crossed their chests.

Gregorio regarded the policemen suspiciously. "Do we have to worry about them, too?"

Fermin made a sound of dismissal. "Contraband is still of no interest to them. They are here simply to keep the peace."

Gregorio flinched at the use of the word *contraband*. "I don't trust anybody anymore. We had better make sure we talk in Basque."

When they had finished their soup and half the bottle of wine, Gregorio began to relax. "How many horses were you able to get?"

"Fifty head."

"Are they any good?"

"Forty-nine are *rocinantes* and the fiftieth is a joy to see," said Fermin. "A beautiful animal."

"Did you have to steal him?"

Fermin's moustache bristled. "I'm not a thief," he said, offended. "I bought him with the rest."

"Where did he come from?"

"Well, it occurs sometimes. A pretty foal out of a *rocinante*."

"I was joking with you," said Gregorio. "I joke because I'm feeling better."

"Well, I'm happy you are feeling better," said Fermin. "But I'm not a thief."

"Let it go," said Gregorio. "I apologize to you. Are the new men as mud-footed as the horses?"

"I insist they are passable animals. If you want to walk a little, you can take a look at them."

"Let it go," said Gregorio. "Obviously, this is not my day for making myself understood."

"You can appraise the men without having to walk," said Fermin. "They are sitting behind you."

"Is that a good idea?" asked Gregorio. "All of us together in a public room?"

"What difference does it make? There are no secrets in this village." Fermin regarded him with concern. "You're changing, Gregorio."

The smuggler sighed. "It's just that I feel everybody is working against us these days."

"You may be getting old," said Fermin. "It's only a suggestion, but perhaps you should start training your son to run the business."

"Now it's you who must be joking."

"No. I'm speaking honestly."

"Didn't you know?" asked Gregorio. "My son is in seminary. He's going to be a priest."

Fermin whistled softly. "What drove him to do that? Especially with such a business to inherit."

"He did it to absolve my sins."

"That must hurt your feelings."

"No," said Gregorio. "I always like to have insurance."

Fermin pulled at his moustache reflectively. "You may be right. Perhaps I should have a talk with my sons. Except that none of them seem inclined to that kind of work."

"I have someone in mind, however, to run the business," said Gregorio. "Can you guess who it is?"

Fermin knew he was being tested. "Without consideration, I would say your bookkeeper. With consideration, I would probably change my mind."

"Your judgment agrees with mine," said Gregorio. "My bookkeeper is efficient, but he has the imagination of a bookkeeper. So forget about him. I have another man in mind. Do you know Nikolas?"

"Hardly at all," said Fermin. "I have met him on the mountain a few times."

"What do you think of him?"

"I don't know. Nikolas is very quiet."

"That's in his favor in this business," said Gregorio. "But he is also a steady man."

"How is his courage?" asked Fermin. "That is most important."

"As far as I can tell, Nikolas is absolutely without fear. He has never failed me."

Fermin posed the question deliberately. "Is Nikolas very poor?"

"Why do you ask that?"

"The prospect of sudden riches can do funny things to a man."

"We were poor when we began," said Gregorio.

"Yes, we were poor," said Fermin. "But in modesty, riches

have not affected our judgment. With others we know, it has not always been so."

Gregorio was silent for a while, then said, "Nikolas is very poor. In fact, he is one of the poorest men I know."

When Fermin called his men and the recruits over to the table, they brought their chairs with them. The policemen in the corner of the room watched the movement without interest and went back to talking.

Except for a short nod of greeting, Gregorio did not involve himself in the guarded conversation. Fermin repeated his instructions to the new recruits, and they repeated questions they had asked before. From a tactical point of view, the exchange was of no benefit to Gregorio. This time around, the recruits from Spain would have the easy task. The contraband horses were being smuggled into France, so the affair would be of little interest to the Spanish *carabineros* in their outposts in the mountain passes. What was smuggled into France was not their concern. Once the horses had been delivered at the right time and right place on the French frontier, the contraband became the problem of the French frontier guards. It was their duty to confiscate merchandise being smuggled into France. And the problem of how to avoid the French frontier guards would be for Gregorio's man, Nikolas, to solve.

Fermin's men knew that they were being appraised by Gregorio. And he in turn was being appraised by them. Gregorio's masked gray face did not reveal a clue as to what he thought of Fermin's men. He had already decided he could find nothing to complain about.

Instead, Gregorio was amusing himself with the thought of how alike the smuggler's breed was. Good chests and strong legs, a little hunger and an elastic conscience. A doubt furrowed his brow and as quickly disappeared. Out of all that he knew about his own man, Nikolas, it had occurred to Gregorio that he had never considered the matter of how elastic Nikolas's conscience was.

The old peasant in the corner had turned his chair around so that he could see better. His arms were folded across his chest and he had settled back to watch the conspiracy. He had a cast in one eye, and the dull light from the window made it gleam wildly. There was a smile on the peasant's face. The conspiracy was a diversion he had not anticipated.

2

Gregorio the Basque smuggler arrived with the beginning dusk at the outskirts of his own village of Donibane in the French Pyrenees. He had driven all the way from the restaurant westward to the Bay of Biscay before recrossing the frontier into France at an altogether different location. He had also taken pains to make sure he was recognized at both the Spanish and French customs stations. Not that it mattered, but he wanted to create a little confusion among the frontier guards. From the baffled expressions at the customs stations, he knew he had succeeded. The telephone lines along the frontier would be very busy that day as the French frontier guards tried to figure out approximately where and when Gregorio's contraband would be coming into France.

Gregorio's villa lay in a secluded park on the far side of the village of Donibane. He did not go there directly. Instead, he turned off the highway and followed narrow lanes flanked by berry bushes and upright slabs of stone that served as fences. He encountered no one of importance, only a quartet of children with fishing poles who scurried aside and an old Basque peasant who stared at the car with surprised eyes and a gaping mouth.

The farm that Nikolas occupied as tenant lay at the base of a wooded mountain nearly two kilometers from the village. It did

not consist of much—a house and a barnyard surrounded by a
lone cornfield and a hayfield that also served as pasture after it
had been mowed. The house had long since surrendered to
time. Its shabby stone front could not remember its last coat of
whitewash, and the decorative wooden timbers were crumbling
with rot. The manger was affixed to the house in the old
manner. Its doors hung askew, and hogs and chickens and
ducks came and went freely. A hunting dog ducked his head
and bayed Gregorio's arrival, then went cringing to him for the
expected pat on the head.

The wife of Nikolas appeared in the blackness of the doorway, made an involuntary movement of retreat, and then came
out into the yard. She was a thin, tired woman who was growing
old too quickly. Still, there was enough of the coquette left to
make her push at hair that had not been combed since last
Sunday. At her heels trailed two children in faded smocks and
smudged faces that had probably not been washed since last
Sunday, either.

"*Bonjour, monsieur,*" she said, extending a damp hand.
"What a surprise to see you! Come in, come in."

Gregorio found that he was looking for signs that he had not
looked for before. Her welcome was warm, but her momentary
apprehension had not escaped him. He answered her greeting
and, despite his impatience, followed her dutifully into the
house. From long experience, he knew that the amenities
became more important in ratio to a person's poverty.

One huge cave of a room served as kitchen and dining room
and parlor. Nikolas was nowhere in sight, but it was too soon to
bring that matter up. The woman brushed the crumbs off a
chair, and he sat down at the scarred wooden table. A clean
tablecloth and a bottle of vermouth materialized beside him.
Smells from the interrupted supper preparation mingled with

the pungent animal odors that seeped from the adjoining manger. They were not unfamiliar to Gregorio. He remembered them from his childhood without regret.

The two children were observing him from a distance with great round eyes. The woman ordered them away, but Gregorio said, "No, let them be. They're not bothering me."

The presence of the children gave the woman an opportunity to talk about something in particular. She had already exhausted the inquiries about his own family's health, her voice faltering a little when she asked about his son's progress in seminary.

Scrubbing at her children's faces with her apron, she said, "They are not pretty to look at today, but I do what I can. The work comes first, you know. And the good Lord knows I don't have a maid to help me." She intended this as a joke, but it was not successful.

"The children will be of help soon," said Gregorio. "As soon as they're old enough."

"As soon as they're old enough, they're going to America," she pronounced firmly. "What chance is there for them here?" She began to intone, "The poor stay poor, and the rich . . ." Thinking better of it, she did not complete the phrase.

"And what will they do in America?" asked Gregorio without interest.

"They will get rich," she said passionately. "The boy will become a great *patrón* of sheep, and the girl will marry a millionaire!" Ashamed at her emotion, she added, "It's not impossible, you know. It has happened before."

"No, it's not impossible," said Gregorio. To himself, he thought, *Merely improbable.*

"And then they will come back and take care of us in our old age," she said. The words had been said so many times that they took on the cadence of a chant. "We will have a rich farm and Nikolas will have *domestiques* to help him with the fields and I will at last have a maid. And we will all live together in happiness."

Gregorio was becoming uncomfortable. "By the way, is Nikolas about?" he ventured casually. "I would like to say hello before I leave."

She accepted the subterfuge with poorly concealed apprehension. "He's in the cornfield. You know how it is with Nikolas. Never a moment of rest for him." She hesitated, then added her own subterfuge. "If you want to stay inside where it's cool, I'll send the boy to fetch him."

Gregorio stood up without obvious haste. "The air will do me good," he said. "I don't get much chance to walk anymore." He caught the fleeting bitterness in her eyes that said, *Well, thanks to you, that's something Nikolas doesn't have to worry about.*

The children had edged closer to Gregorio. Not wanting to let the conversation end there, Gregorio dug into his pocket and came up with two coins. He asked the children to hold out their hands. When they did not respond, he repeated the demand in a firmer voice. Two palms were extended timidly, and he placed one coin in each. The tiny fingers closed over them like traps. He waved aside the woman's pleased objections and took his leave, wondering how much Nikolas's first decision to become a smuggler's man had to do with his wife's lamentations about poverty.

Gregorio found Nikolas at the dividing line between the cornfield and the pasture. The cart with great wooden wheels was nearly filled with corn. The oxen had been unhitched and turned into the pasture, still yoked together.

Out of the habit of his own years as a smuggler's man, Gregorio approached Nikolas soundlessly along the rows between the towering cornstalks. But Nikolas heard him anyway. He was leaning quietly against one of the great wheels in an attitude of waiting. The fine debris from the cornstalks covered his face with powder, and the powder was cut through with rivulets of sweat. He had a long, fleshless face and unrevealing blue eyes. Despite the torn shirt and beret and shapeless cotton pants, Gregorio was again struck with Nikolas's dignity. If poverty had touched this man, he did not reveal it.

"*Adio,* Nikolas."

Nikolas made a nod of his head. "*Adio.*"

Gregorio went to lean against the cart, too. They stood side by side without looking at each other. The narrow valley stretched below them, a sweep of green fields and brown fields cut into jigsaw shapes by hedgerows and stone fences, whitewashed farmhouses with mottled roofs of blackened tile and new red tile, all converging upon the white village commanded by a church steeple.

Gregorio reached into the deep pocket of his tweed coat and took out a crumpled pack of cigarettes. He offered the pack to Nikolas. Each lighted his own cigarette. In the still air, the thick smoke from the black tobacco lifted as lazily as in a closed room. Gregorio surveyed the cornfield in which they stood. "You've got good corn this year."

"Yes, it's a good crop," said Nikolas. "I have no complaints."

"How much do you get to keep?" asked Gregorio.

"Two-thirds of the harvest," said Nikolas. "One-third of everything goes to the *propriétaire.*"

"That's a heavy share for him."

Nikolas laughed shortly. "And a light one for me. I don't have to worry about a profit."

Gregorio watched the smoke from his cigarette climb into a dusk made grayer by lowering clouds. "I'm afraid we're going to have some bad weather."

Nikolas surveyed the cloud bank. "Well, at least we will have it tomorrow."

"No longer than that?" asked Gregorio.

"Perhaps it will last through tomorrow night," said Nikolas. "But not much longer."

"It will be just fine if the weather stays bad through tomorrow night," said Gregorio.

Nikolas was silent for a moment. "How many head?"

"Fifty."

"Mules?"

"No. This time, horses."

"For a passage of fifty animals, I would have preferred mules."

"So would I," said Gregorio. "But the demand is for horses."

Nikolas shrugged. "Well, we can't have cake every day."

"You will need four men to help you," said Gregorio. "Can you get them in a day?"

"I think so," said Nikolas. "Tomorrow is market day, you know. Everybody will be in the village."

"All of your helpers, too?" asked Gregorio.

Nikolas nodded. "I've been going through it in my mind. Justin and Andres have pigs ready to sell, Joanes has a veal, and Luis will be there in any case."

Gregorio deliberated for a moment and then decided to be tactful. "I know Luis is brother to your wife, but if you're worried about his temper, I can get you somebody else."

"Luis has a temper," said Nikolas, "but he is faithful to me. That is more important."

Gregorio snorted derisively. "And besides, he needs the money to pay for the drinking he would like to do." Pushing himself away from the cart, he turned to face Nikolas. "I accept your judgment," he said evenly. "But for your sake as well as mine, keep Luis close to you. I want no incidents with the frontier guards. Despite anything else they say about me, they cannot say I've ever broken the accord with a single incident of violence. If you are caught, leave the damned horses and run like hell. And make sure Luis doesn't stay behind to cause trouble with the guards."

Nikolas met his gaze. "There's been no trouble on any passage I've led. You have nothing to complain about."

With one corner of his mind, Gregorio had been observing the yoked oxen in the pasture. Turning their locked heads to right and left, they were feeding in perfect unison. Though each must have had his individual desires in the matter of feed, there was never any pulling in opposite directions. One was the unquestioned leader, and the other the follower. It was as simple as that. Gregorio asked quietly, "Are you trying to make an argument with me?"

"No, *patrón.*"

Gregorio was amazed. He had thrown out the challenge of a proper master. Nikolas had delivered the response of a proper minion. But he had done it with absolutely no subservience. There was neither anger in Nikolas's blue eyes nor insolence in the set of his mouth.

"My name is Gregorio," he said harshly. "From you, the word *patrón* is not to my liking. If you like the title so much, you can have it for yourself."

Nikolas's long herculean frame stiffened so imperceptibly that Gregorio would not have known it except for the starting of the veins in the great arms.

"Are you mocking me?" Nikolas asked quietly.

"I am not mocking you," said Gregorio. "If you can make this passage for me with success, you will become my partner in business."

Nikolas regarded Gregorio with bafflement. "I don't understand what you're saying."

"There's nothing to understand," said Gregorio. "When you get back, we will talk about the arrangement."

"But what can I offer you?" Nikolas asked. "I am only a peasant."

"You are deceiving yourself," said Gregorio impatiently. "You are more than that, and you know it best of all. I was a *peasant*, too. But obviously, I am not one anymore. What you are now is of no importance to me. What is important to me is that you have the makings of a good *contrebandier*."

For the first time that Gregorio could remember, Nikolas's level gaze wavered. "I don't know," he said unevenly. "I don't know."

"What's bothering you? The prospect of having a lot of money?"

"I haven't had much experience with money."

Gregorio grimaced. "It's a disappointment to me when you say foolish things. What are you really afraid of? The shame of being known openly as a smuggler? Even if you've managed to keep what you are doing a secret, you're a little bit pregnant already, you know."

"I know that."

"What is it, then? Are you afraid of the loss of your good name?"

"No."

"Yes," said Gregorio. "Don't worry about hurting my feelings. I've lived long enough to learn the lies in life. Because you have been clever enough to work in secret, you can consider yourself respectable. But are you really more respectable than I in your heart?" Gregorio aimed a finger at Nikolas. "Listen to me. I am a known *contrebandier*. But when I invite the mayor to dinner, he comes to dinner. When I invite the priest, he comes to dinner, too. Do the mayor and the priest come to your respectable house for dinner? When I go to a bistro, the men of the village do not ignore me. The rich drink with me because I am rich, too. And the poor drink with me because it's good to know a man with money. I'm telling you something now. What we call respectability is a foolish little game the poor must play in order to hold themselves equal to the rich, who are seldom respectable. And the proof of it is this. I may be a *contrebandier*, but when I'm dead, I will be remembered longer and better than the priest."

Gregorio paused only once as he made his way through the field. He had neglected to tell Nikolas that the frontier guards would be on alert for a movement of contraband. He considered retracing his steps, but only for an instant. Fifty animals and four men and a new proposition for living added up to a sufficient burden for Nikolas. Anyway, it was a wide frontier.

3

When the rain on the roof became an insistent drumming, Nikolas roused himself and looked up as if expecting to see the rain falling out of the darkness above his head.

In the diminishing glow from the fireplace, the children were playing jacks with a rubber ball and the rounded backbones of a lamb. His wife was mending a rent in a short cape the color of night. But Nikolas had been watching neither of these activities. Without being aware of it, he had been staring for a long time at the place on the stone floor where his wife's feet rested. The rope sandals that enclosed them were shredded and black with dirt.

Nikolas had made it known by two oblique actions that there was a trip to be made. He had built a fire in the grate and he had demanded wine with his dinner. He sat now at the wooden table, from which the tablecloth had been removed, his hand circling his glass. The table was just beyond the arc of light from the fireplace, so that he observed a stage of his own making from the darkness.

He had revealed nothing to his wife, but his trips in the night were never discussed between them. He simply went, and, sometime before dawn, he came back. The next day, there was extra money in the brass pot on the mantelpiece. In this way, he

imagined she was at least spared the burden of knowing exactly
where the money had come from. It was a thin subterfuge, but
for a woman whose good name was about the only thing in
which she could have pride, it was better than no subterfuge at
all.

It was surprising how few people really knew. He believed
this was because he had moved so discreetly and chosen his
men so carefully. Even in the village, he had searched behind
people's eyes for a sign that they knew he was a smuggler's man.
He had found it only in the families of those who were his
helpers, where it was a safe secret. Then again, perhaps the
villagers knew and didn't care. No one seemed to hold it against
a poor peasant for being a smuggler's man. It was so little
money, anyway, and it was not like stealing from a neighbor.
The only victim was the government, and who had ever felt
sorry for a government? And he had not broken the unspoken
rule against rising above the station to which he had been born.

But if he accepted Gregorio's proposition, that would be
another matter. Then he would have broken the pattern in a
land where patterns were not made to be broken. If your father
was a cobbler, then it followed that you were a cobbler. If your
father was a peasant, then you had better remain a peasant, too.
If you were born poor, then it was your duty to remain poor.

But what about those who had broken the pattern? Men like
Gregorio, or better yet, those few who had actually come back
from America to live. Men who had gone away poor and come
back with money. People talked about them, too, calling them
Amerikanoak and not Basque anymore simply because they had
gone away. People remembered when the *Amerikanoak* had
lived in poverty and held it against them for getting rich in
another land, all the while forgetting that it would have been
impossible for them to do so in their own land. Still, when the

time of adjustment was past and the remarks became so tired
that no one made them anymore, one practical fact remained—the *Amerikanoak*'s new station in life.

Perhaps Gregorio was right, after all. He and his wife and
children had suffered the barbs, too, but the fact of their new
station in life still remained. Perhaps respectability really was a
foolish little game, after all, and money was the only thing that
counted. A man could not feed and clothe his family with the
substance of respectability, but he could do it with money.

Nikolas had come to know that if people did not gossip about
you for one thing, they would gossip about you for another. The
more important you were in wealth and station, the more
people would gossip about you. It was simply a condition of life.

But somewhere, something was missing. Gregorio lived in
luxury and talked as if he had come to peace with the world.
Then Nikolas remembered Gregorio's son, who had also lived
in luxury and yet had gone to a barren seminary in an act of
atonement for his father's profession. Gregorio could joke
about that, too, but Nikolas wondered how deep the joking
went. In one way, Gregorio was right. People would remember
him longer than the village priest. In another way, he was
wrong. They would not remember him better.

Nikolas regarded his own son in the waning glow from the
fireplace. The game was over, and the boy had gone to sleep
beside his sister on the stone floor. He was lying on his side, one
hand thrust awkwardly into the pocket of his soiled smock.
Nikolas felt a rush of affection for the tiny circle of his family
and a deep satisfaction at the decision he had come to in his
mind.

Then the sleeping boy rolled over on his back, and the hand
that was thrust into his pocket came out and opened. The
shining coin that had been clasped there rolled across the stone

floor and disappeared into a deep crack. The wife of Nikolas let out a cry of rage and loss and scrambled from her chair in hopeless pursuit of the coin. The boy woke up in sudden comprehension and stared at his empty palm as if it were a traitor.

Outside the circle of light, Nikolas raised his eyes from the scene that had unfolded itself before him, destroying forever any illusion of the true circumstance of his life. The upper darkness descended like fate upon his head, and the rain beat down with the sound of relentless drums.

The remarkable thing was that Nikolas was not at all surprised to see them. But this was because he could say to himself, *I am merely dreaming that I am a boy again, and you are pretending because you do not exist, and I am pretending because I know you do not exist.* All he would have had to do to dispel them was to fix his attention on the feel of the rippling grass that caressed his bare feet and the breeze that brushed the fringe of hair over his forehead, or to raise his eyes to the ordered line of poplars along the edge of the lane and the neat hedgerow and upright slabs of stone that divided this meadow from the field where his father was following behind the oxen with his wooden plow.

So, knowing that it would be a simple matter to dispel them, Nikolas was not afraid. Instead, he submitted to them.

If Nikolas had been standing up instead of lying down in the meadow, the knoll would not have reached higher than his knee. And if he had spread his coat, it would have completely covered the patch of velvet grass on the crest of the knoll.

The little man dressed in black from his beret to his sandals was the first to appear. The little man did not even seem to notice Nikolas's presence. He was too filled with self-importance. Striding imperiously to the crest of the knoll, he surveyed the patch of velvet grass as if determined to find a fault in it, then retired to one side to seat himself upon a stone. When he sat down, he made an elaborate show of straightening the folds in his black cape. And when it was finally draped to his liking, he sighed. Raising the tiny silver flute to his lips, he blew one long piping note like a signal.

In their own way, the dancers were as vain as the little man with the flute. But then, they had reason to be. Their costumes were so resplendent that, for an instant, Nikolas believed he was seeing rainbow reflections of sunlight on dew.

The first dancer to come onto the knoll was holding aloft a wisp of crimson cloth on a sliver of wood, and he led the others onto the patch of velvet grass. He was followed by one who seemed to be a man, yet his movements were those of a woman. He had on the brilliant blue tunic of a man, braided in patterns of silver and gold, but beneath that, he wore a red skirt and the tiny white apron of a woman. He had a flagon and a goblet in his hands. Detaching himself from the rest with mincing steps, he set the goblet down in front of them and, with solemn ceremony, poured wine into it.

The next to appear also seemed to be a man. He was dressed in the scarlet tunic and yellow knee breeches of a man, yet walked with the sinuous movements of a cat. He was carrying something, too, zigzag wooden scissors nearly as long as himself.

When the last dancer came over the crest of the knoll onto the patch of grass, the others bowed their heads in deference. He was unmistakably a man, with the towering headdress and scarlet tunic and black breeches of a warrior. Around his waist was the wooden frame of a miniature horse with silver reins and rich caparisons of white lace. His bearing was princely, and his

costume so altogether dazzling that the others faded into in-
significance beside him.

When the dancers were assembled, the little man with the
flute struck another piping note in signal that the performance
was about to begin. As the note died away, the dancers recognized the presence of Nikolas in the deep grass for the first time
and, turning in his direction, bowed gracefully. But when
Nikolas laughed out loud in childish delight, the little man with
the flute glanced at him in annoyance, as if to say, *This is a
business of life, not at all to be laughed at.*

The little man with the flute began to play, and the music
was like the shrilling of a hundred birds. At first, it seemed to
have no meaning at all. It was wild and abandoned, and
because it occurred to Nikolas that he had heard it somewhere
before, it was also disturbing.

But if the music in itself had no meaning, the dancers made
meaning out of it. Where the music was wild, their movements
were as restrained as those of puppets. From the waist up, they
held themselves rigidly erect, so that their flashing feet did not
even seem to belong to their bodies.

The standard-bearer was the first to approach the wine goblet. He did so proudly, with tiny sandals skimming so close to
the goblet and over its surface that it trembled where it stood.
The dancer with the man's tunic and the skirt of a woman was
next. Though he performed the same steps, there was an
underlying caution to his movements, so that the goblet did not
tremble even once.

Watching them, Nikolas was so enchanted with the beauty of
their dancing that he did not attach much importance to the
presence of the goblet. But when the dancer with the wooden
scissors approached the goblet and began to clip the air above it
as though cutting away invisible threads, Nikolas began to grow

fearful. There was a meaning to the goblet of wine that he could not comprehend.

When the dancer with the scissors had finished, the music suddenly stopped. There was an instant of silence, and then one piping note. It had hardly died away when the little man with the flute burst into shrilling notes that were wilder than anything else that had gone before. But in that instant of expectant pause, Nikolas noticed for the first time that all the dancers except the resplendent warrior with the miniature horse carried tiny *poignards* in their belts.

In time to the music, the dancers came forward together. Flanked by the others, the warrior was the only one to approach the goblet. He did so with haughty disdain. His feet were a blur of movement, coming so close to the goblet that it seemed to be constantly trembling. It seemed unbelievable that he could tempt fate any more.

Then, as if that were not enough, the warrior suddenly leaped with one sandal onto the goblet itself, and then away. No sooner had he done this than he leaped onto the goblet with his other foot, and again leaped away. The goblet rocked, but it did not fall.

The dancers retreated together, but only for a moment. Watching them, Nikolas's heart began to pound violently. He knew what was to come. He could not watch that great a risk. But he could not take his eyes away.

The resplendent warrior approached the goblet for the last time. He did so alone, but with a confidence so supreme that it was painful to see. The flute shrilled louder, the tiny sandals moved faster, darting to one side of the goblet and then the other, and then over it. Suddenly, the warrior was in the air. He came down on the goblet with feet together. They rested on the edge of the goblet for a fleeting instant, then the dancer leaped

high into the air and away. The goblet rocked to one side, teetered, and fell over. The wine spilled out in a red stain onto the velvet grass.

The music stopped. The dancers recoiled, their hands in the air, their mouths open in horror. Stripped of his confidence, the warrior stared unbelievingly at the overturned goblet. The dancers screamed once in outrage. Then, with *poignards* glinting like needles in the sunlight, they descended upon the warrior. Headdress and braided tunic and white lace crumpled into an unproud heap on the grass, and blood ran out in crimson streams to mingle with the wine.

4

The clip-clop of shod hooves and the rumble of the cart were drawing nearer on the lane behind him. The calf that Nikolas was leading had come along docilely enough, but now Nikolas was forced to contain the animal's antics.

The cart drew alongside Nikolas and slowed to a walk. It had red wheels and red sideboards, and a fat pig reclined on a bed of clean straw inside it. The cart was led by a mule whose coat had been clipped on top and was long-fringed on the bottom, like an upside-down haircut.

"*Adio, adio, adio,* neighbor!" said a merry voice. "What perfectly villainous weather, eh?"

The man had a round face so pink that little veins showed through on his cheeks. He wore a wool coat of quality and polished brown boots of French leather, and he spoke from under a huge black umbrella that protected him like a tent.

Nikolas returned the greeting, but could not pay attention because of the bucking calf. He shortened his grip on the cord and took a firm twist in the calf's tail with his free hand. The bucking subsided to little hops.

"He's a pretty calf," said the man on the red cart. "It's a shame you have to walk him. He'll be four kilos lighter by the time you get to market. You should have stopped by my farm. I could have brought him in the cart, you know." He paused, then said brightly, "In fact, if you want to put him in . . ."

"Thank you, but no," Nikolas interrupted. "It's only a few steps more."

"Well, I had better be going along," said the man, flicking his reins. The mule moved off at a reluctant trot, then was hauled back again to a walk. "I want to ask you something. What are our selling prices for animals today?"

"I don't know," Nikolas called after him. "I haven't talked to anybody. I don't know what the others have agreed upon."

"*Adio!*"

Nikolas watched the red cart until it had disappeared around a bend in the lane. The calf quieted down, and Nikolas let go of his tail. The rain had seeped through the doubtful thickness of the coat that had been part of his wedding suit, and his father's before him. He debated opening the umbrella whose curved handle was hooked in back onto the collar of his coat and decided it was not worth the trouble. The village was very near, and he would need both hands to control the calf.

For the tenth time that morning, Nikolas regarded the sky. The day had dawned bleak and wet. The first force of the storm had passed, and the rain had settled down to a fine drizzle. Clouds hung low over the village and the valley, obscuring the mountains beyond. Nikolas guessed with satisfaction that a man would have trouble seeing twenty paces up there.

At the last knoll, the lane changed from a dirt path to a cobblestone street that dipped sharply down into the heart of the village. Below him, the winding main street was a tumult of bleating sheep and squealing pigs and bawling calves. Peasants in black berets and sombre clothes tugged and kicked and swore at their animals, and those who had pigs were doing most of the swearing. A buyer's truck that had arrived late was trying without success to honk its way through the street. One man had lost his footing on the wet cobblestones, and his pig was dragging him along on his stomach. A path opened up miraculously in front of the charging pig, and a roar of laughter marked the owner's sliding passage. When the incident had gone on long enough, two men leaped at the pig in an attempt to drag it down. One came too close and was bowled over like a tenpin, but the other managed to grasp an ear and twist it. The pig skidded to a stop, and its owner sat up to nurse his bruised elbows and shake his fist at the onlookers.

Nikolas watched in amusement until the man had gotten to his feet. At least he had broken no bones. Taking a double twist in his calf's tail for safe measure, Nikolas descended into the street. Aside from bawling in outrage, the calf made his way with little resistance to the buyers' station. Nikolas found a stall with only two calves inside and tied his animal to the railing. There was a buyer regarding him. He was a little man with smoothly combed hair and thick glasses and had an extravagant array of pencils in the breast pocket of his long gray smock.

"Do you call that a veal?" the buyer said. "He would make a better suitcase."

Nikolas shrugged and said nothing. He knew that his calf was a good one, and the jibe was proof that the buyer knew it, too.

Ignoring Nikolas, the buyer turned his attention to a woman leaning possessively against the same stall. She was dressed in widow's black, and she was the only woman visible in the entire street. She had a pinched face and wispy gray hair, and one last tooth clung stubbornly in the front of her mouth.

The buyer was haranguing her in French. It was an old ploy but an effective one. The buyer was more fluent than she in French. But she was not to be disadvantaged and answered him stubbornly in Basque.

"Don't talk to me in Basque," the buyer said. "It touches my heart and makes me soft."

"It might make you soft," the widow sniffed, "but there's no danger it will make you honest."

The buyer looked offended. "I don't have the habit of lying, madame."

"Then why don't you offer me an honest price for my veal?"

"It is an honest price," the buyer said. "I am within the range of today's accord on price."

"Yes, but at the bottom of the range," the widow said. "My calf should be at the top of the range."

Throwing up his hands, the buyer walked away. The widow jerked her chin up and down in triumph, as though she had won the argument. But Nikolas knew differently. In the end, the buyer would have the last say, for one simple reason. He knew that she needed the money.

The men were gathered under a large cluster of umbrellas against the side of an old stone rampart, and Nikolas opened his own umbrella and went to join them. There were a few murmurs of greeting, but not much conversation. It was too early in the morning for that. The conversation would come later at lunchtime, when there was wine on the table and money in their pockets. They stood for the most part in stolid silence, some with cigarettes dangling from their mouths and all with faces burned by cold and rain.

After a while, Nikolas asked, "What is the accord on prices today?"

A peasant with a striped blue coat handed down from another generation related the prices as if by rote, and Nikolas said, "They're not good."

"That's no surprise," said the peasant. "They are always too low. We ought to take our animals and go home."

Knowing this was a threat without substance, Nikolas did not bother to take it up. He pretended to watch the buyer who had insulted his calf. The buyer was probing with his fingers along the backbone of Nikolas's calf. Satisfied with that, he lifted the tail to judge by what he found there if the calf was indeed a veal that had been fed by milk alone. The buyer seemed satisfied and Nikolas knew he would offer a good price before the morning was over.

Making a show of nonchalance, Nikolas surveyed the crowd of men. Justin and Andres, his helpers on movements of contraband, were standing together at the far edge. Glimpsing Nikolas's approach, they turned as if by a common signal. Justin nodded slightly, but, after the first glance, Andres pretended to be occupied with something on the ground. Nikolas had begun to saunter in their direction when the sound of Luis's raised voice came clearly to his ears. He paused apprehensively. There was an argument going on in the crowd, and Luis was part of it.

Because Luis was family, Nikolas did not need to pretend concern for him. He shouldered his way unceremoniously through the knot of peasants that surrounded Luis and his antagonist. From the low-keyed but deadly snatches of language, Nikolas realized instantly what the argument was about. Some man had broken the peasants' united front on prices, and Luis was taking him to account.

Nikolas burst through the ring of men too late to thwart the first blow. The peasant who had broken the accord was staggering backward with his hands raised in front of his face. He was a foot taller than Luis, but thin as a rake, and the blow had caught him on the side of his beaked nose. Blood jetted from his nostrils, but the nose was not crushed. Luis was preparing to rectify that. His bull shoulders were coiled for another blow, when Nikolas's arms closed around him and lifted him into the air.

If it had been anybody else, Luis might have broken free. But after one contorted glance at the face of the man who held him, Luis gave up the struggle. Nikolas propelled him through the ring of men and set him down well away from the peasant who had broken the accord. Even then, Luis was not ready to abandon the argument.

"What do you think of a man like that?" he cried through bared teeth.

"Let it go!" said Nikolas. "He's learned his lesson. Do you want to kill him?"

"By God, that's a good idea," said Luis, making a move as if to break away.

Nikolas seized him by the arm and, drawing him close, hissed into his ear like a rebuking parent. Luis's attitude changed instantly. As comprehension dawned, his brow cleared and he grinned delightedly. "Why didn't you say so in the first place?" he cried.

In a harsh whisper, Nikolas told Luis to lower his voice. His gaze swept over the faces of the watching men. If they had attached anything out of the ordinary to Luis's words, their faces did not reveal it. But then Nikolas caught a movement on the walkway above the rampart. Raising his eyes, he saw the figure of Gregorio poised there. The smuggler's face was averted, but there was cold anger written in every line of his body.

5

"What is it to be this time?" asked Justin.

"*Rocinantes*," said Nikolas.

"How many?" asked Andres.

"Fifty."

Luis gave a low yelp. "Fifty!" he said, rubbing his hands together. "That's more like it. The old pirate is beginning to show some style."

Joanes, a wiry little man who was another of Nikolas's helpers, had joined them.

"A pity it's not catching," he said caustically to Luis.

Nikolas and his helpers were eating lunch in a little restaurant with low ceilings and red beams running into whitewashed walls. The restaurant was filled with men sitting with their elbows planted firmly beside their plates and berets still on their heads. The smell of wet wool coats mingled with the scents of food and wine and brandy.

Precisely because of Luis, Nikolas had chosen a table at the open window that looked out over the river. With his other helpers, he could have conversed in the middle of the street without arousing suspicion. But Luis was another matter.

Still, nobody in the marketplace seemed to have attached too much importance to Luis's act of violence. The low roar of a waterfall overrode the sounds of the restaurant, confining conversations to individual tables. Enough wine had flowed to make the talk boisterous, and singing had already broken out at one table.

Justin and Andres were two of a kind, unmistakably brothers, with grave eyes and blade-like faces so narrow that a child's hand could span their foreheads. In the manner of their mountain family, they spoke but little, with no words wasted.

Joanes was like them in some ways, but he had traveled much. He was a little man with a wiry endurance that contradicted his several missing teeth and graying hair. Within the limits of his ability, he had attempted many things and had either failed or grown weary of them. He had tried to be a handball player, but all it had gotten him was a few crippled fingers. He had fought with the French military in Algiers, and he had been wounded. He had gone to America to herd sheep and come back with neither money nor the language. Out of all his experience, he had acquired only an attitude of cynicism and a taste for whiskey.

After Joanes's rebuke, Luis had assumed an air of sulkiness. But Nikolas knew it would not last long. Luis had the emotions of a child, ranging unrestrainedly from uproarious laughter to terrible violence. But unlike a child, all this was enclosed in a brute's body of massive bones and slabs of muscle.

Using the pretense of pouring wine, Justin asked quietly, "When is the passage to be?"

"Tonight," said Nikolas.

Justin paused in his pouring. "Then we had better take it easy on this."

"It would be a good idea," said Nikolas.

Luis made a sound of disgust and reached for the abandoned bottle. "Speak for yourselves," he said, filling his glass to the brim. "It's a long time until tonight."

"And a longer night," said Joanes contemptuously. "You would do better with sleep instead of drink."

"At your age, yes," said Luis. "But I am not your age."

"Haven't you caused enough trouble for one day?" Joanes retorted. "If Nikolas had not stopped you, you would be in jail by now." Joanes would have gone on, but he saw that Nikolas was regarding him with disapproval.

"I would like to see the jail that can hold me," Luis scoffed.

"You will find it one day," said Joanes.

As if the two brothers' thoughts had been transmitted to each other, a faint annoyance reflected itself simultaneously in Justin's and Andres's eyes. "Do we have to talk about jail?" said Justin.

"Why not?" said Joanes philosophically. "It's better to get used to the idea. One of these times . . ." he began, then shrugged and let it rest there.

"I know someone who doesn't have to worry about jail," said Luis with bitterness. "We take the risks and he takes the money."

"That goes with being the *patrón*," said Joanes. "You would do the same if you were in his shoes. So would Nikolas and so would I, except that I have no stomach for such a responsibility as money."

Luis laughed aloud. "Nikolas a *patrón*? That will be the day."

"Why not?" said Joanes. "It could happen. Gregorio is getting no younger."

"Don't forget that Nikolas is my relative," said Luis. "I know him better than you do."

Joanes was regarding Nikolas quizzically. He looked away when Nikolas met his gaze, but not before there was an instant of communication between them. "Perhaps you do and perhaps you don't," muttered Joanes.

So the wise one of my helpers suspects something, thought Nikolas. Despite the quick clamping of his stomach, he was surprised to find that Joanes's knowledge did not trouble him nearly as much as he had imagined. "There are other things to talk about," he said with unaccustomed harshness. Leaning across the table, he began to relate Gregorio's instructions for the night's passage.

He was nearly finished when he felt the sharp nudge of Justin's foot against his ankle. Abruptly, the table fell silent. Joanes yawned and stretched elaborately. Luis scraped a match and touched it to the dead cigarette in his mouth. Like twins, Justin and Andres merely looked grave.

"What am I interrupting here?" intruded a voice blurred with wine. "A conspiracy?"

"Yes, as a matter of fact," said Luis. "We are conspiring to rid the country of landowners."

"That kind of joke doesn't amuse me," said the intruder. "You talk like a communist."

"Do you want to see me?" said Nikolas to the man who was *propriétaire* of his farm.

"What kind of price did we get for our veal?" the *propriétaire* asked imperiously.

When Nikolas told him, the *propriétaire* said, "You could have done better." He paused and asked as if in afterthought, "Do you have the money with you?"

"Of course," said Nikolas.

"Then I will take my share of it now."

Nikolas stared at the bloated face. "No, you will not."

The *propriétaire* made an effort to focus his eyes sternly upon Nikolas. "What are you saying?"

"I am saying you have no right to interrupt my dinner with such a demand."

"You're talking pretty strong."

"That may be," said Nikolas quietly. "Now, will you excuse us? We have something to discuss."

The *propriétaire* was preparing to make an argument out of it when he noticed that Luis was regarding him in a peculiar way. Turning on his heel, he moved off unsteadily.

"He will make you suffer for this, Nikolas," said Justin.

"Then he had better enjoy it while he can," muttered Nikolas. But, except for Joanes, the remark went unnoticed by the others.

Luis was absorbed in thought. "You know," he said. "Your *propriétaire* has given me something to think about. Maybe I will become a communist."

"Then it's good-bye for the Basque country," said Joanes. "As a dictator, you would give Stalin a run for his money."

"Stalin is dead," said Andres.

"That's a shame," said Luis. "I would have liked to talk with him."

A serving girl with black hair approached the table. "Do you want anything else, *messieurs?*"

Luis reached out a hand toward her leg. "Not the others, but I do."

She slapped his hand away with composure. "I can believe that."

"Will you be at the dancing tonight?" said Luis.

"No," said the girl. "I'm going to bed."

"Alone?"

"Of course alone," said the girl. "I'm not married, you know."

"What a waste," said Luis.

"If you feel that way, why don't you do something about it?" said Nikolas when the serving girl had gone.

"If it were up to me, I would," said Luis. "But her father doesn't consider me a gentleman."

"What an insult," said Joanes dryly.

"No, I'm not insulted," said Luis. "I have my youth to think of. When I begin to feel old, then I will entertain the idea of being a gentleman."

"If you live that long," said Joanes.

When they emerged from the restaurant, the afternoon market was in full activity. The winding street was lined with vendors' stalls offering fruit and vegetables and squawking chickens and frightened rabbits to the village dwellers, rough work clothes to the peasants, cotton smocks and dresses to women, and footwear of approximate fit and doubtful quality to everyone.

With market baskets in hand and colored umbrellas over their heads, farm women and village women alike wandered through the winding aisle of stalls, visiting with each other and bargaining with those vendors who were Basque. There was a sprinkling of gypsy vendors in the street, dark-skinned men hawking their wares with pretended warmth and resentful eyes. With them, the Basque women would not demean themselves by the ritual of bargaining. Their only bond was what a gypsy had to sell and the Basque women wanted to buy, and only one price was mentioned.

Nikolas had been observing a woman make her way down the street. She was dignified, with a handsome face and gray hair combed neatly back into a bun. She wore a subdued suit of soft wool with a scarf of fine silk about her throat. It was Gregorio's wife. And though she stopped often to visit with women in the street, it occurred to Nikolas that she went her way alone.

There was a sudden murmur of conversation among the men standing in front of the restaurant, and Nikolas turned to see what had caused it. He did not have to look far. A convoy of three olive-painted jeeps was making its way slowly through the throng in the street. There were four men and one police dog in each jeep. The men wore blue uniforms with a long red stripe running down the side of the pants. They had on rough mountain boots and wore scarred holsters at their hips. The dogs were the huge, midnight-black descendants of the German occupation.

"Ah, hah!" chortled a peasant who was standing next to Nikolas. "Reinforcements! The mountains will be busy tonight."

Nikolas heard an obscene curse from Luis and the voice of Joanes, overriding him before he could go on. "Personally," Joanes said loudly, "I am opposed to this display."

"For what reason?" asked the peasant suspiciously.

"Because it is a waste of time to send all those men up there," said Joanes.

"What does that have to do with you?" asked the peasant.

"As a taxpayer," said Joanes, "I consider it a waste of my money."

"You may be right," said the peasant. "I've never thought about it that way."

Nikolas's eyes met those of the others. Justin and Andres were sombre, and it would have taken someone who knew them very well to detect the fact that they were worried. Luis's lowered brow was sullen, and Joanes wore a studied air of unconcern.

Nikolas extended his hand. They touched fingers as if in ordinary parting, and turned wordlessly away from each other.

6

It was so dark that he could have gone forward into the clearing between the two stands of forest without fear of meeting anyone. Still, Nikolas stood for a long moment under the protecting trees and listened. The leaves above his head were heavy with water, and great droplets accumulated on them and spilled down onto his beret and the coarse blue cape that covered his shoulders.

Directly in front of him there was a patch of vineyard, neat rows of wooden crosses draped with gnarled vines. In the darkness, the vines took on the shapes of men, so that the vineyard resembled an orderly army of cripples supported by crutches.

Beyond the vineyard stood the last of the outlying farmhouses. The house was a chalky smudge against the backdrop of black forest, and one lone window was framed forlornly with light. Inside the farmhouse, a dog barked once and fell quiet, as though unsure of what he could sense but not smell. Nikolas moved quickly, skirting the vineyard and the barnyard beyond. By the time the dog's barking started up again, Nikolas had crossed the road and plunged into the trees on the other side.

There was a covering of newly fallen leaves on the forest floor, but they were sodden with rain and muffled the sound of his passage. When he had left the farmhouse far behind, he slowed his pace and began casting about for the hidden trail through the bracken. He found it without difficulty and began the long climb. He had known the narrow trail since his childhood, and its turns and dips were as familiar to his sandaled feet as any street in the village. Even in the falling darkness, he knew when he was passing a giant oak whose ancient and fearsome branches he had climbed as a boy, or a stand of beech trees with trunks encrusted with gray lichen, or the ravine where a streambed had knifed its way through the trail. Here, he was forced to wade into chilling water up to his knees.

When he could taste vapor in his mouth and nose, he knew he was entering the low-hanging cloud bank. Now, his vision was totally obscured by the mixing of night and mist. He guided himself by walking only where the trail remained firm beneath his feet. He climbed cautiously but steadily, pausing as the trail grew steeper to gain his breath through the filter of scarf that he had wrapped over his nose and mouth to protect his lungs from the vapors.

When he could no longer feel the presence of trees nearby, he knew he was reaching the edge of the timberline. The trail and the forest ended decisively, and now there was grass beneath his feet. The darkness had lessened, and the night had taken on a cast more gray than black. The day would have revealed an absolutely treeless sweep of rolling hills and shallow ravines covered with a solid mantle of grass.

Nikolas stood and listened patiently to the silence. When he was satisfied, he cupped his hands to his mouth and hooted once like an owl. There was a moment of waiting, then an answering hoot. It came from the proper direction, and Nikolas made his way to its source.

In a hollow above the timberline, there was an abandoned shepherds' hut. One side of its slate roof had collapsed, but the other remained precariously intact. When Nikolas stooped to enter the low doorway, he saw by the glow of cigarettes that there were two people inside the hut. They were huddled out of the rain under the fragment of roof.

"Is everyone here?" asked Nikolas.

"Just me and my brother," said Justin miserably.

Finding his way with his hands, Nikolas squatted down beside them. The wall of little stones fitted together was like ice against his back.

"A fire would be welcome," he said.

"We considered it and decided no," said Justin.

"You were wise," said Nikolas. "It would be too much of a risk. Did you see any movement by the guards?"

"Neither a light nor a motor," said Justin. "But then, we came by the forest instead of the road."

"I would hope so," said Nikolas. "They will be patrolling tonight, for certain." He shivered once with the cold. The figure beside him moved, and Nikolas felt the touch of leather against his hands. "Here," said Andres. "It will dry you inside, at least."

Nikolas unscrewed the cap from the nozzle of the goatskin gourd and upended it. Despite the darkness, the jet of wine found his mouth and seeped warmingly through his body.

They sat in silence, listening to the rain on the slates. "We're running late on time," said Andres judiciously.

"Not too late," said Nikolas. "But Joanes and Luis should be arriving together any minute now."

"Perhaps," said Andres.

Nikolas detected the note of doubt in his voice. "What do you mean by that?"

Justin interceded for his brother. "We heard the barking of a dog."

Nikolas was silent, trying to decipher what the brothers were not saying. "You mean a guard dog?"

"Yes," said Justin.

"Where did you hear him?"

"While we were coming through the forest," said Andres evasively.

Nikolas allowed impatience to show in his voice. "I gathered that," he said. "But from what direction did the barking come?"

There was another silence, then Justin said with reluctance, "From the direction of the road."

"Do you mean to say Luis and Joanes took the open road?"

"I don't mean to say anything," Justin said defensively. "All I said is that we heard the barking of a guard dog from the direction of the road."

Nikolas suppressed an uncommon anger. It was far too soon for the searching guards to leave their jeeps and penetrate the forest on foot. They knew as well as the smugglers exactly what was involved in the movement of contraband. What they did not know was the time and the place of the passage. They patrolled simply on the off chance that they could surprise a man walking where it was not reasonable for him to be walking. If there had been barking from the direction of the road, then it was probable that Luis and Joanes had been foolish enough to take the open road and walk right into the hands of the guards. If that had happened, it was of no importance whether they admitted anything to the guards. The fact of their presence on the road was admission enough. The guards would be assured that the passage was to be tonight and not one week from tonight.

When Nikolas spoke, his voice was matter-of-fact. "Are you up to handling fifty horses?"

"Are you joking?" said Justin.

"No."

"There are only three of us!" Andres protested.

"Do we have any other choice?" asked Nikolas, getting to his feet. "Joanes and Luis have probably been taken by the guards. In any case, we can't wait all night."

"We could wait a few minutes," said Andres. "They might have gotten away."

In answer, Nikolas went through the low doorway and began walking.

They had passed over the bare hump of mountain that marked the frontier. France was behind them and they were descending the Spanish slope. For a while, at least, they did not have to worry about detection. This was the no-man's land where the French patrols were prohibited from entering and the Spanish *carabineros* were not concerned enough to venture, particularly in a storm.

On the lofty rim of the mountain they had observed with uneasiness that the storm was beginning to dissolve. The clouds that had shrouded them so completely on the ascent from the timberline had become visible wreaths, and they caught occasional glimpses of stars overhead.

The knowledge that he had predicted the brief duration of the storm to Gregorio was small consolation to Nikolas. As things stood now, the dissipating storm compounded the obstacles posed by only two helpers and the fact that the French guards had been alerted. In normal situations, Nikolas could predict the attitude of the French guards toward a combination of night and bad weather and black forests. This had always been the main advantage the Basques held over them. Smugglers were willing to endure cold and wetness, and they knew the depths of the forests better than the guards ever would. But it would be another matter if the storm spent itself too soon. The woods would be infested with guards, and the movement of fifty horses would be about as discreet as the passage of an army. More than ever before, the possibility of capture on the return trip loomed distinctly.

How ironic it all was! How many passages had he made with the threat of capture hanging over him at every moment? And if he had been captured, it would all have been for nothing except a few pieces of money. In those times, his usefulness to Gregorio would have ended abruptly, and his only rewards would have been prison and disgrace. One day ago, he had been ready to turn down Gregorio's proposition because of the single drawback of being known as a *patrón* of smugglers, with no risks involved. He had changed his mind, only to be ensnared in a predicament where if he were caught, it would mean not only prison and disgrace, but the end of all opportunity.

Hearing the sounds of Justin's sopped sandals behind him, Nikolas turned his head to observe the black-garbed shapes of the brothers. He realized with a quick shame that he had not thought once of their welfare or that of Luis and Joanes, but only of the night's application to his own future. Something within him was changing. He did not know exactly what it was, but he knew that he was not the same man he had been yesterday.

They had descended the slope and were approaching the Spanish timberline. There was a smell of wood smoke in the air and a fixed glow somewhere beyond the first curtain of trees. As they drew nearer, they heard the sounds of horses milling heavily in an enclosed space. A figure made huge by a long cloak stood waiting for them at the edge of the forest. A flashlight flared in their faces and instantly went out. The sodden figure stepped aside.

"*Pasatu*," an unhappy voice said in Basque.

7

The tiny cabin was crowded with men. It was a woodcutter's cabin, square and high-raftered, and the planking on the walls was saturated with the odors of cooking grease. Except for a table and a bench and a straw pallet, the room was bare. There was a fireplace at one end, and the heat from the oak fire blazing in it was almost more than the room could support.

The fire and a smoking kerosene lantern on the table provided the only light. At first, Nikolas could make out nothing except dark shapes sitting on the wooden floor or slouched against the walls. The uncertain light glinted off a cheekbone, the bridge of a nose, the knuckles of a hand. Then, slowly, he made out a few faces he knew, others that he did not know, and a man with flaring moustaches who was sitting alone and in authority on the wooden bench.

"Did you have a pleasant stroll?" the man with the moustaches called out. There was a murmur of laughter in the room, and Nikolas remembered him as Gregorio's man in Spain.

"Come over and dry out," said Fermin, gesturing to the fire.

The men sitting on the floor shifted over, and Nikolas and the brothers made their way to the fireplace. They stood with raw hands extended to the flame and their backs to the room.

Water dripped down from their capes, forming pools on the oaken floor.

"One would think it was raining tonight," said a young voice.

"What a foolish idea," said another man. "It never rains in Spain."

"That goes without saying," said the young voice. "But they have come from France, where it always rains."

"And only three of them at that," said another man. "What confidence!"

"But everyone knows three French Basques can do the work of seven Spanish Basques," Justin said sarcastically.

"Take a drink," said Fermin, interrupting the banter. "There is Pernod and Spanish brandy."

Nikolas turned away from the fire. "Pernod," he said. He looked at the brothers. "For all of us."

"You," said Fermin to a young man sitting near the table. "Make them a drink."

"I am a smuggler," said the young man, "not a waiter."

"*Merde*," said Fermin. "Your work is over for the night. Theirs is just beginning. Make them a drink."

The young man got up wearily and poured Pernod and water into tin cups, then sat down again. Nikolas stepped to the table and took the cups.

Fermin glanced at the door of the cabin. It had been closed firmly behind the three men. "Are your comrades outside?"

Nikolas did not look up from his cup. "No."

Fermin regarded him with incredulity. "Three men for fifty horses? You are very sure of yourselves."

"We were five to begin with," said Nikolas.

"Also, the French guards are alerted," said Justin bitterly. "They have reinforcements."

There was a silence, then a low whistle from someone in the room. "Do you mean to say your comrades have been taken?" asked Fermin.

"These two heard the barking of a guard dog," said Nikolas. "What else is there to assume?"

"Assume?" said Fermin. "Didn't you come together?"

"Separately to the shepherds' hut," said Nikolas. "The French guards work harder than yours. We have to split up and come separately to avoid the risk of all of us being taken together."

"To say that French guards work harder than Spanish guards is not so," a voice interjected.

"There are no finer guards in Europe than our Spanish guards," said another man indignantly.

"There are no finer guards in the *world!*"

"*Merde*," said Fermin, but no one heard him. The room had dissolved into argument. He sat in silence on the bench, pulling at his moustaches and staring at the floor. After a while he heaved himself to his feet and went to Nikolas, his massive back toward the room. "It is impossible for me to lend you any men," he said in a low voice. "If they were caught, the French would send them to prison and throw away the key."

"It doesn't matter," said Nikolas.

"How will you go back?" asked Fermin. "Do you have a plan?"

Nikolas nodded, and Fermin felt an instant withdrawal in the man. After a moment, Fermin said with authority, "I am involved here, too. What are Gregorio's instructions?"

Nikolas regarded him impassively. "Same as always. Follow the frontier to Iraty forest and go down from there."

Fermin almost let it go at that, then a thought furrowed his brow. "And is that what you plan to do?"

"No," said Nikolas quietly. "We are going back by the same route we came up. The guards would never expect us to do that."

There was a sharp exclamation of protest from Justin. "What are you saying, Nikolas!"

When he realized no further explanation was forthcoming, Fermin said, "I see what you are intending. Surprise. However, you are taking a lot upon yourself."

"That is my burden," said Nikolas. He gulped down the remains of his drink, stepped past Fermin to set the tin cup on the table, and began threading his way among the men on the floor. Justin and Andres exchanged glances and then looked to Fermin as if for intercession. Fermin shrugged and turned away from them. Before, he had not been certain whether Gregorio had broached his proposition to Nikolas. He was uncertain no longer.

The French frontier lay less than a stone's throw in front of them, along the rim of mountain that reared jaggedly into the night sky. Still, they waited in the deep shadow under the shoulder of the mountain, each with his string of gaunt Spanish horses tied head to tail in single file.

It was necessary to wait. The last shreds of the storm were passing over and the sky was brilliant with stars, and they could not risk an instant of exposure on the skyline. Finally, in the distance, Nikolas saw what he had been waiting for, a remnant of cloud large enough to conceal their dash over the rim. He watched its approach, judging its size by the stars which were blotted out in the sky behind them.

"Be ready, now," he called out in a low voice.

Justin and Andres did not answer. They stood apart from him

in the same angry silence they had maintained during the return to the frontier. There had been a moment outside the woodcutter's cabin when the brothers had almost deserted Nikolas. Because they had never been confronted with trouble of such magnitude before, they were suddenly unable to consider alternatives. They could not divorce themselves from the formula that a smuggler came up the mountain by one route and returned by another. Because the return route through Iraty forest had been clear before, they were absolutely unwilling to believe it would not be clear again. It was typical, the peasant's trait of clinging to the established order of things. But Nikolas had never recognized it so clearly.

In the end, he had managed to convince Justin and Andres to follow him, but it had taken some doing. He had tried to explain that the smallest concentration of guards would be on the route where Luis and Joanes had been seen. The three men would at least have the element of surprise.

The remnant of cloud was nearly above them. Nikolas tightened the halter rope in his hand. "Now!" he called out. There was a succession of jerks against the rope, and then the string of horses behind him was in motion.

They crossed the rim of the mountain in perfect obscurity. The trailing veil of the cloud held them until they were over the skyline and well into the concealing darkness of the other side. The cloud went scudding off toward the black line of forest far below. Nikolas paused only once for a rapid survey of the plain. In the starlit night, the great grassy sweep glistened with wetness. A thousand tiny hillocks crouched like gnomes upon its undulating surface. Behind him, a horse chose this moment to splash urine. Apart from that and the labored breathing of men and horses alike, there was neither sound nor light anywhere below.

A chain of shallow ravines flanked the high plain. It was marked by a single stream that wound like quicksilver to the forest. Nikolas led the way into the first ravine. The grass beneath their feet was spongy with rain, and one horse stumbled on the slippery surface and fell heavily. Nikolas waited until it had floundered to its feet and then went on until they found the firmer path that bordered the stream. Occasionally, there was a clatter of stones set loose by weary hooves, but the rushing sounds of the stream muffled that, and the long descent was made with little enough noise.

The chain of ravines emptied out near the abandoned shepherds' hut that had been their rendezvous. They were almost abreast of the hut when a low whistle brought Nikolas up short. He stopped so quickly that the horse he was leading snorted in fright. Reaching up, Nikolas caught the animal by its halter and covered its nose with his hand. The horses behind quieted submissively.

At first, Nikolas thought that one of the brothers had signaled him. But when he looked back, he saw that the caravan was moving steadily forward. Wheeling, he faced the dark outline of the shepherds' hut. A figure in a beret detached itself from the shadow of the hut. In a moment, it was followed by another. Nikolas did not need to hear their voices. With a sinking in his heart, he realized that the two figures were Luis and Joanes.

"My God!" Andres cried hoarsely. "What do we do now? The forest will be crawling with guards."

"This is what comes from changing plans," said Justin. His voice was heavy with accusation.

"But I tell you, we weren't seen," Luis protested.

"But they knew you were there," cried Andres.

"What difference does it make?" said Joanes disgustedly. "We might as well have been seen. The guards knew their dog was after something."

"It could have been a hare," said Luis. "It could have been anything."

"When does a hare kill a dog?" said Joanes with contempt.

"What did you expect me to do?" Luis protested. "Let him tear me apart?"

"There are other ways to fight a dog," said Joanes. "You didn't have to kill him."

"How do they know he's dead?" said Luis. "They'll never find him in that forest."

"They don't have to," said Joanes. "When he didn't come back, they knew."

Luis turned to find Nikolas. "You should have seen me. The way I took that dog. I was magnificent!"

"Yes," said Joanes. "Magnificently stupid."

"Do you want to get killed?"

Nikolas stepped between them. "That's enough!"

Until then, Nikolas had not said a word. Standing in the shadow of the hut, he had let the argument rage around him. There was no other course. It was a foolish argument over deeds that could not be undone. It was also a waste of precious time, but, in the end, he hoped that the venting of spleen would steady them. He barely listened. In a detached corner of his mind, he was seeing them as he had never seen them before. He was seeing them in crisis, and it was laying them bare.

He had always regarded Justin and Andres as completely dependable. Now the imminence of trouble had brought out sides to them that had been hidden behind their quiet gravity. Fear had made Andres frantic, and Justin, antagonistic and blaming. Luis was not afraid, but he was no better for it. The

violence in his nature had made him a single agent in what
should have been a team, unable to see the consequences to the
rest in what he had done. Only Joanes, with the soldier's
training in him, had remained constant. With him, it was
merely a question of impatience with stupidity.

"If you're through arguing," said Nikolas, "it's time to go."

"Not by this route," said Justin fervently.

"What other way is there?" asked Nikolas.

"The way we've always gone before," said Justin.

"Even if you were right, it's too late for that now. The night is
almost gone."

"Then I say we turn the horses loose," said Justin. "By
ourselves, we can get out."

"Do you know what you're saying?" said the soldier in Joanes.
"Desertion!"

"Desertion from what?" Justin scoffed. "What does Gregorio
care if we go to prison?"

"I would hate to have you with me in war," said Joanes.

Justin was beyond being stung. "I owe nothing to Gregorio!"

Joanes took a deep breath. "You owe something to Nikolas."

"Nikolas has nothing to do with it," said Justin.

"Do you want to tell them, Nikolas?" asked Joanes.

There was a silence. Nikolas decided suddenly that he would
tell them nothing about his new arrangement with Gregorio.
"No," he said curtly.

Something fell into place in Justin's mind. He grunted as if
he had received an unwelcome blow. When he spoke, his voice
was defeated. "All right, we'll come. But I warn you, Nikolas.
Even for you, we will not be captured. If there is even the smell
of trouble, we'll run."

"Justin!" Andres cried out in protest.

Nikolas clasped Justin by the shoulder. "That's understood. Run like hell."

A glimmer of comprehension had pierced through to Luis. "You could have told me, Nikolas," he said reproachfully. "After all, I will be your partner."

"Shut up," growled Joanes. The black forest below them had taken on a new menace, and he suddenly understood why Nikolas had nothing to tell. If they were caught by the guards, Nikolas would lose more than they.

8

In the stillness of the clearing, the shot was like the splitting roar of a cannon. The shot and the spurt of flame into the night sky and the bounding black dog came together. The horse that he was leading reared up with a shrill scream. Nikolas stumbled backward, and then the dog was upon him.

In an instant, the night was filled with the pounding hooves of terrified horses and the startled shouts of men. Locked with the dog, Nikolas found himself at the bottom of the melee. A glancing blow from a hoof struck his shoulder, but he barely felt it. The impact of the dog's rush had hurled him to the ground, and he had thrown up his arms to protect his face from the ripping teeth. He heard the dog's snarling, then a chance glint of light illuminated the yellow eyes of the beast. The sight filled Nikolas with fury. Reaching up with one hand, he caught the dog by the loose skin of his throat and pushed him away. His fist swung in a sweeping arc and crunched home against the side of the black head. The dog shuddered, and Nikolas swung again. Shoving the limp form aside, Nikolas began to scramble to his feet.

"Don't move! You are a prisoner!"

Nikolas sank down on his knees. Out of the corner of his eye, he saw the outline of two booted legs planted firmly beside him.

He did not need to look up to know that a gun was pointed at his head.

Then suddenly, there was a tremendous crashing of bodies, and the booted legs were gone as if they had vanished into thin air. A shot exploded almost in Nikolas's face. He heard a great grunt of expelled air, then a pistol miraculously appeared on the ground in front of him. He leaped to his feet.

Afterwards, Nikolas would remember that he saw everything an instant too late. He saw the frontier guard lying pinned on his back on the forest floor. He saw the white blur of the guard's face and the great staring eyes. He saw the black-cloaked figure straddling the guard and knew immediately by the massive shoulders that it was Luis. He saw a poised hand and the coldly shining knife it held. He heard the single protest that was his own voice, and the animal gurgle of the guard's severed life. The blur of face on the ground was white no longer, but black with blood. Luis was kneeling over him, a bloody knife in his hand.

Joanes was standing beside Nikolas now. He was breathing with great difficulty. Somewhere from the black wall of trees that surrounded the clearing came the sound of men and dogs searching without caution through the tangled underbrush.

"They are closing in on us," said Joanes.

"The others?" asked Nikolas huskily.

"Gone at the first shot."

"The horses?"

"Gone, too."

Stooping, Nikolas picked up the guard's pistol and held it cradled in his open hand. The barrel that rested against his fingertips was warm. He felt a surge of sickness rising from his stomach.

"We don't need that," said Joanes.

"We don't," said Nikolas. "But Luis does."

Luis had not moved from where he knelt. He was staring at the knife in his hand as if he could not comprehend what it had accomplished. Nikolas laid the pistol on the ground beside him. Luis turned his head to regard it and then looked up at Nikolas.

"Are you leaving me?" he asked, and his eyes were like the eyes of a child.

"You know the rules," said Nikolas.

"But it was for you, Nikolas."

"You went too far."

Nikolas and Joanes had fled far enough down the hidden trail that they could no longer hear the guards searching the forest. But not far enough to avoid hearing the crack of a single pistol, the instant of silence, and the thundering flurry of shots that followed.

Gregorio opened his eyes slowly and blinked into the darkness above his bed. The sound did not come again, and for a moment he believed that he had heard it in a dream. He made an effort to recall what the dream had been about, but there was not one lingering thread. The thought struck him that this was in itself odd, but he was not disposed to ponder on it in the middle of the night. Heaving himself over on his side, he closed his eyes and proceeded to go back to sleep.

When the sound came again, there was no mistaking it. The flat crack of the door knocker on the floor below reverberated through the silent house. Even before its echo had died, Gregorio was out of bed and groping for his trousers. He pulled them on hurriedly, stuffing his long nightshirt into the waistband. The heavy gold watch he carried in his trousers had a luminous dial, and he tilted it back and forth until he could see the hands. It was not the middle of the night, after all, but a few minutes short of four o'clock.

His wife had awakened and was sitting up in bed. There was a time when her voice had always carried apprehension. But that time was past. "Do you want me to turn on the light?" she asked calmly.

"No. Go back to sleep."

Outside the bedroom, a small balcony overlooked the front entrance to the villa. Gregorio opened the French doors, slid back the bolt to the thick wooden shutters, and stepped out through the aperture he had made. The night air was moist and fragrant, but, above all, cold. Shivering, he glanced at the sky. The storm had passed, and the sky was filled with stars.

He leaned over the balcony railing. "Who is it?" he called down in a loud whisper.

There was a crunch of footsteps on the gravel below, and a figure emerged onto the driveway. "Nikolas!" a voice whispered back.

It was as Gregorio had anticipated. "I'm coming down," he muttered resignedly.

Without haste, Gregorio closed the shutters and the French doors and sat down on the chair. His slippers and heavy black shoes were lying side by side. He chose the security of the shoes, lacing them tightly to his feet. His wife's head was on her pillow, but he knew by her breathing that she was not asleep.

Despite his attempt to walk softly, the heavy shoes clumped outrageously on the wooden staircase. Then Gregorio remembered there was no danger of waking his son anymore, because his son was gone. Gregorio forgot about the noise he was making. He felt a sudden ache of emptiness within him and made an effort to attribute it to the early morning hours he so despised. That and the prospect of bad news.

The foyer was dark, but the cold blue light filtering through the stained-glass windows in the heavy door enabled Gregorio to see well enough. He turned the key in the lock and peered outside, but there was no one on the porch. It was a moment before he saw that Nikolas was still standing in the driveway.

"What in the name of God are you doing out there?" he asked irritably.

Nikolas stepped up onto the porch. "I'm filthy with mud."

"I'll try not to notice," Gregorio said dryly. He led the way into the kitchen, went to the window to make sure that it was shuttered, and turned on the light. It was a huge kitchen, white-tiled and gleaming with conveniences. Gregorio went into the dining room beyond and returned with a bottle of brandy and two glasses. Motioning Nikolas to the table, he filled both glasses to the brim. "Drink up," Gregorio said. "I have a feeling we're both going to need it."

Gregorio permitted himself to look at Nikolas for the first time. What he saw confirmed his fears, and more. The long face was streaked with mud and stubbled with beard. Gregorio had expected that. It was also drawn with exhaustion, but Gregorio had expected that, too. He had not expected what he saw in the blue eyes. They were not the eyes of anyone he knew.

Whatever anger Gregorio was prepared to feel was dispelled. "So the government of France is richer by fifty horses today than it was yesterday," he said, rocking back in his chair. "So there will be an auction and I will buy them back at no loss except my profits for the year." It was the closest he could come to sympathy.

Nikolas roused himself. "I had better tell you what happened."

"The details of what happened are of no interest to me now,"
said Gregorio. "The affair is terminated, and you had better go
home before you drop dead from fatigue."

"You have to know."

"I told you . . ." Gregorio began, then fell silent with an inner
knowledge come home.

"A guard has been killed."

Gregorio's chair came down with a crash. The gray mask
disintegrated. "Who? Who? Who killed . . ." Then Gregorio
knew. He stared wildly at Nikolas. "I warned you! I warned
you!"

"Luis is dead."

Gregorio groped for the bottle. With utmost care, he took out
the cork, filled his glass, and raised it to his lips. By the time the
ritual was completed, at least his outward composure was
restored.

"Tell me."

When Nikolas had finished, Gregorio was silent for a long
while. His voice was matter-of-fact. "It's better than the guillo-
tine."

"Yes."

But something was missing from Nikolas's terse account.
Gregorio deliberated before asking the question. "Who ordered
Luis to stay behind?"

"Me."

"You?"

"Yes."

Gregorio stared in wonder at the floor. Now he understood
what had happened to Nikolas's eyes.

Day had broken and the cold light of dawn had been dispelled by a brilliant sunrise. From the balcony outside his bed-room, Gregorio watched the caravan of horses and guards and jeeps moving in procession past his villa and onward to the village.

The older guards among them did not even take the trouble to acknowledge the presence of Gregorio's villa. But some of the younger guards cast resentful glances as they passed by, and one went so far as to make an obscene sign. But that was the way with youth, and Gregorio was not surprised by it. In time, they would learn that in this, as in all matters, an accord must exist. The game that had been played that night was an old, old game, and the most youthful of the guards were much too young to understand that the only important thing was that the code of a death for a death had been satisfied.

In the village, the early-rising shopkeepers would find cause for merriment when the contraband horses began to troop by. They would be more discreetly amused about the weariness of the frontier guards who followed. And they would be sobered with the aspect of the final jeep and the blanket-wrapped bodies lashed to its hood. The surmise and the speculation would keep them occupied for many days.

Gregorio wondered if any of the surmise would touch Niko-las and decided that it was unlikely. But within the circle of his family, it would be another matter. When the first grief had subsided, there would be recriminations. Gregorio did not envy Nikolas his homecoming.

Because Nikolas was the kind of man he was, Gregorio was curious how he would survive the experience. Then he remem-bered what had amazed him only a few hours before. For a man to pass sentence of death upon a stranger was one thing. But to have done it to one of his own family was another. What a general the man would have made.

Because of what had happened, Gregorio had abandoned the idea of making Nikolas his partner. He had been prepared to tell Nikolas tomorrow that the new arrangement was off. But now, he was not so certain. Gregorio decided that he would wait at least until the day after Luis's funeral. By that time, both he and Nikolas would know their minds very well, indeed.

9

They faced each other across the grave like enemies.

Nothing had been said until now, when the proprieties were done. But it had not needed to be said. Through the preparations and the vigil, the saying of the Mass, and finally the burial, Nikolas had known it was coming. He had seen it in the bent, condemning figure of Luis's mother, the cold wrath of the father, and the smouldering hostility of Luis's brother.

The last of the mourners and the black-cassocked priest were trailing through the cemetery gate. The priest had lingered a little longer than the others, as though puzzled about something. But in the end, he had left the grave and the forbidding circle of the family, too.

"When I think of his poor body . . ." Luis's mother moaned, moving her hands as though probing for holes.

Nikolas stood alone on one side of the grave, his hands clasped awkwardly in front of him, staring at the ground. His wife was a little apart from him at the foot of the grave, as though uncertain whether she belonged with her family by blood or with him. "It's done now," she said apprehensively. "Luis is dead. It's better to forget."

"It's not done," the mother spat out. "It will never be done!" This was the beginning she had been preparing all along.

"Such a good boy," the father said. "So young, so kind. And now he is taken from us." His voice began to tremble. "By the tempting of another."

Nikolas raised his eyes. "Luis came with me of his own free will."

They had been waiting for him to speak. Through the angry protests, the mother's voice cut sharply. "He came because you were his sister's husband. Because of that, he thought he owed you loyalty."

"It had nothing to do with my wife," said Nikolas.

The mother drew back her lips to reveal toothless gums. "Your wife!" she said with bitter contempt. "She is your wife in name only. She is our blood, not yours. Thank God for that."

"Shall we fight over a blessed grave?" pleaded Nikolas's wife.

"He gave you loyalty and you repaid him with death," the father said to Nikolas.

"Someday I will learn what happened up there," said the brother. "And then you, Nikolas, had better watch out."

"Are you threatening me?"

For the first time since they had known Nikolas, they saw in his eyes the capability for murder. Their anger retreated, but something else took its place. In the silence that followed, the wife of Nikolas moved quietly to his side. But when she lifted her head and looked upon her family, there was a faltering within her.

"Will you come now to our house?" she asked her family. It was a last, hopeless plea.

"You will never see me under your roof again," the mother said coldly.

"Nor your husband under ours," said the father.

"If my husband is not welcome," said Nikolas's wife, "then neither am I."

"As you will," the mother said.

The father shook his head as though stunned at an un-expected turn of events. He turned to his wife imploringly and found only the iron of finality. His son passed in front of him and led the way to the gate. The mother hobbled after him. In bewilderment, the father began to follow, then he wheeled to face Nikolas.

"You!" he gasped. "You were not content to be what God ordained you to be. You have destroyed my name and my family. May God repay you for that."

"Now I have lost them forever," said the wife of Nikolas.

In the silent cemetery, Nikolas held the woman who was now truly his wife. He felt the sobs that wrenched her body, but he could not hear her words.

He was remembering an afternoon when his life had changed. It was a lazy afternoon in summer, and he had come out in the front yard to sit for a while in the shade of a tree. The sky was a blazing blue, the shade was cool, and he dozed to the sound of insects droning in the air. He was quite asleep when a cry from the children roused him, and he opened his eyes to see the gray figure of Gregorio approaching him across the yard.

In that first meeting, Nikolas remembered that his choice had been made from need of money. He had sensed that he was stepping outside the prescribed circle of his life but banished the apprehension that the step was fateful. And in the meetings afterwards, Nikolas had reassured himself time and again with the thought that the hesitant first step could be revoked whenever he wished. He had not known then that it was already too late. He had ventured outside the prescribed circle. After that, there could be no return.

In this, at least, his wife's father was right. And Nikolas wondered what form the payment would take.

10

The building that housed the headquarters of the frontier guards was distinguishable only by the French tricolor hanging limply from a short pole over the doorway. It was an unpretentious building so little cared for that the white plaster had dropped away in places to reveal bare patches of irregular stone beneath.

As was the case with other buildings that housed the offices of functionaries, the headquarters fronted on the wide and cobblestoned village square. Three stone steps led up to the doorway, so that anyone standing on the top step commanded a view of the village square.

The chief of the local detachment of French frontier guards stood on the top step. He was a tall man inclined to stoop in his private moments, and his military moustache was liberally streaked with gray. He stood erect now with a dignity he did not feel.

The chief had been stationed in this post long enough to recognize the faces that looked up at him from the village square. Through the years, he had seen most of them a hundred times. But that was as far as it went. He knew their faces, but he did not know the people.

The chief held no rancor toward the Basques for this state of affairs. On the surface, they were cordial enough. But they were also a separate breed who thought and acted in ways that were incomprehensible to a Frenchman. The chief was looking forward to his retirement in the north of France.

The auction that he was about to conduct would amount to nothing more than a farce, and he would emerge from it feeling like a fool. Whether the auction was for contraband horses or mules or Spanish lace or Spanish wine, it made no difference. The villagers came to watch, but never to bid. In the Basques' own way of doing things, it was simply forbidden to do so. The only serious bid could come from the particular smuggler who had the misfortune to lose his goods.

The chief was privately irked with Gregorio. As with the other smugglers, he had hoped the matter could be settled without the foolishness of an auction. Gregorio could simply have paid a call to headquarters, mentioned that he had heard some contraband horses were to be auctioned, asked to examine the horses, and then made an offer. There would have been a little bartering for show. After that, Gregorio would take his horses, the French government its money, and the affair would be closed.

Perhaps it was the incident in the mountains that had altered the procedure. But that was settled now, and it had been settled according to the code. The young smuggler had been properly buried in the village cemetery, and the new guard from the seacoast had been buried elsewhere, and the slate had been wiped clean. Because he knew Gregorio was not a man of violence, the chief could not hold him accountable for the act of a troublemaker. It could happen to anyone in a position of authority over men.

Something else was afoot, but the chief could not divine what it was. He had learned to see through the inscrutability of the villagers enough to sense that they did not know what was afoot, either. Their presence at the auction revealed that. The butcher had wandered over from his shop in his blood-smeared apron. The day was still young enough for the little drunk of a tobacconist to make it over to the village square under his own power. The brute who owned the popular cafe was there with his long-suffering wife. Even the mayor had come, smiling and nodding to one and all with his eternal greeting of *mon vieux*.

There were some peasants about, but not many. The chief was surprised to see the sister of the man who had been shot, still in mourning, standing at the rear of the gathering. The thought passed through the chief's mind that it was a little early for her to be at public affairs. Beside her stood the fair-skinned giant who was her husband. He was so quiet that one rarely noticed him. The chief could not even recall his name. Then the chief caught sight of Gregorio at the far end of the square. He had driven up in his Citroen and was leaning against its door as if he had no interest whatever in the proceedings.

The chief adjusted his pince-nez and began the ordeal. In a dry, bored voice, he read the details of fact: The government of France was in possession of fifty horses. They were contraband horses that had been intercepted in illegal passage from Spain, confiscated by the frontier guards, and, as dictated by law, would now go to auction. When he was done reading the document, he took off his pince-nez and, steeling himself, asked if there were any bids.

There was a moment of silence and then a voice in the crowd called out, "One franc! I bid one franc!"

The chief did not have to search for the owner of the voice to know that it was the drunken tobacconist. "Is that the worth of your pocketbook?" the chief asked humorlessly.

"No!" the tobacconist shouted. "It's the worth of the contraband."

There was a ripple of laughter, and the chief asked sternly, "Are there any further bids?"

"One franc and fifty centimes for the lot of them!" someone else called out.

As the bidding went up by francs and centimes, the chief raised his head and stared out over the crowd in a wordless plea for someone to come forward and rescue him from this agony. To his immense relief, he saw that a man was making his way through the crowd to make a bid. For an instant, the chief assumed it would be Gregorio. But then he realized he was mistaken.

Leaning against the reassuring luxury of his long Citroen, Gregorio watched as Nikolas glanced back once at the figure of his wife. Her head was thrown back, and she was standing erect. He imagined that Nikolas found strength in that, but it was much too early for Nikolas to see what Gregorio saw—the wall of distance already forming around her.

Gregorio also saw what he suspected Nikolas did not see in the faces that lined his path through the crowd, the whisperings of surprise and the nudgings of scandal, the mayor's new regard and the tobacconist's disdain, one man's envy and another man's hate.

Gregorio saw all this with a pang of things remembered. But the pang was only temporary, and quickly passed.